Jasmine Finds Help

by Marghanita Hughes

WILDWOOD
PRODUCTIONS
PUBLISHING

Published in Canada 2008 by
Wildwood Productions Publishing
www.wildwood-productions.com

Cataloguing in publication data for this book is available
from the British Library.

ISBN 978-0-9546434-4-7

Printed and bound in Canada.

Printed on 100% Post Consumer Waste, old growth free and
chlorine free paper.

WILDWOOD
PRODUCTIONS
PUBLISHING

For my Mother

This book and others in the series are dedicated to
encouraging children to take an interest in
Mother Nature and the Environment.

BOOK 1

Jasmine is a butterfly girl, half human, half bug so she's just like you only she can fly and talk to the animals of the forest. Jasmine and all her Little Humbug friends are the Protectors of Nature.

But the Little Humbugs are growing concerned. So much damage is being caused to Mother Nature and they are working extra hard to keep it safe, but they need help...

Jasmine's mission - to make contact with a human girl.

She finds Lola, could she be the one to help The Little Humbugs!

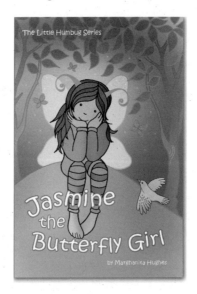

Step into the world of the Little Humbugs. Enchanting forests and sparkling streams, where songbirds sing to the rising sun every morning.

The Little Humbug Forests are filled with Butterfly Girls and Dragonfly Boys. If you are very quiet and respect nature and the animals of the forest you may just see a Little Humbug, taking care of the forest.

The Little Humbugs have been around since time began you just haven't seen them until now.

Chapter One

The clock ticked slowly towards 6 o'clock. Today seemed like the longest day in Lola's life, probably because her two best friends were coming for a weekend sleepover, but this was to be no ordinary sleepover. This was Lola's chance to prove that Jasmine the Butterfly Girl did exist.

You are invited to
Lola's Sleep Over

a special chance to meet
Jasmine
the Butterfly Girl

Love Lola x

Just as Lola was setting out the sleeping bags, the doorbell rang.

"They're here!" she screamed, running to get to the door first, before her little brother, Eddie. They always raced to answer the door.

Lola and Eddie looked very alike; there was no mistaking them as brother and sister with their dark brown hair and warm dark brown eyes. (Lola used to put pigtails in Eddie's hair and pretend he was her little sister until Eddie sat up one day and declared that boys don't wear pigtails, never allowing Lola's hairbrush anywhere near his head again.)

This time, Eddie wasn't about, he was too busy playing with Prince, their new puppy. A mischievous little puppy with bags of energy, he constantly chewed at everything and everyone.

Lola opened the front door excitedly. She welcomed her friends with the biggest smile, rushing them upstairs to her bedroom.

Best Friends Forever

The girls were the best of friends and loved sleepovers. This was going to be the best-ever sleepover, declared Lola, grabbing Emily and Miya's overnight bags and tossing them onto her bed.

Lola's room was quite large since her brother had moved into his own room. They had shared a room up until last month, when Lola had turned eight years old. Her mother, a children's book illustrator, had secretly painted a beautiful mural for Lola as a surprise birthday present. The underwater scene of beautiful mermaids and brightly coloured fish covered three walls of the room. Lola had always wanted to be a mermaid but not anymore; she had other ambitions, and these included flying.

Emily and Miya loved Lola's room, especially the mural. Each would have loved to have one too.

On the fourth wall, Lola's desk, with its secret drawer where she hid her special things, was situated underneath a large window facing the garden and the park in the distance. Lola loved to gaze out at the trees and the birds, imagining all kinds of adventures with her best friends, Miya and Emily.

The girls all went to the same school and lived very close to one another. Miya lived just along the road from Lola in an apartment above the local post office. Although she had no yard or garden, the post office owner, Mr Dodds, a very kind old man, allowed Miya and her sister to grow flowers and herbs in the clay pots

along the entrance of the post office. In spring they filled them with bright red tulips and golden daffodils, and in summer they grew sweet-smelling pink and red roses. The post office always looked so pretty.

Further along the road and over a small stone bridge was a charming old farmhouse where Emily and her family lived. Their house, which had fields on either side of it, was very old. She and her sister went horseback riding at the farm's stables next door.

Chapter Two

As the girls helped Lola set up the beds, Miya enquired, "So when do you think Jasmine will come?"

"I really don't know," replied Lola. "Why don't we make some butterfly-shaped cookies for Jasmine's arrival?" she suggested, trying not to sound too anxious.

"That's a great idea," agreed Emily.

"That's if Jasmine turns up, of course," remarked Miya, following Lola to the kitchen while tying her short blond hair into bunches. She had the most striking green eyes and a sun-kissed face with freckles that spread across her nose, making her look much younger than she was.

Miya was smaller than Emily and Lola and had loads of energy; she never sat still for very long.

Entering the kitchen, they found Lola's mother loading up the dishwasher. The girls pleaded with Lola's mother to let them make some cookies for the sleepover.

Lola's mother kindly took out the cookie cutters and turned on the oven for them. "Don't forget to clean up after you're finished, I know how messy you girls can be," she remarked as she left the kitchen.

"We won't forget," giggled the girls.

Lola kept glancing over at the clock while Emily and Miya measured out the ingredients for the cookies. The time just seemed to go slower the more she looked.

"Pass the baking tray, Lola," asked Emily who was taking control. She tended to be slower than the other two, thinking things through. Being the tallest of them all, with long golden-brown hair and warm hazel eyes, she liked to think of herself as the leader.

As Lola picked up the tray, she caught sight of the sun fading outside. "Look, girls, it's almost time. I'm sure Jasmine will come when it's dark."

The girls hurriedly cut the cookie

dough into butterfly shapes and popped them into the oven. They ran back to Lola's room and stared out of the window. Three little heads popped up from Lola's desk, eagerly waiting to meet the Butterfly Girl Lola had met only a few days earlier.

The sun began to slip slowly behind the distant hills. The sky was a warm pink smeared with soft creamy clouds. As the sun disappeared, the hills became a milky blue outline. The wooded park was almost dark now, and the girls watched for the first stars to appear as the skies grew darker and darker.

Lola couldn't relax. She felt excited but anxious. She was worried that Jasmine wouldn't turn up and the girls would think she had made the whole story up.

As it got darker, the girls got more excited. Suddenly there was a noise, a crashing sound.
"What was that?" asked Miya.

"It's Jasmine. She here!" announced Lola, almost bursting with excitement.

And they ran outside, ready to greet her. BUT NOTHING. Just darkness, then the sound again. As they turned toward where the noise was coming from, something leapt up at them.

"AHH!" they all screamed. Then

looking down, they all began to laugh.
It was only Prince, Lola's puppy. Lola
picked up Prince, they all went back
inside.

Disappointed, they all sighed and
flopped onto Lola's bed.

"Do you think she'll EVER appear, Lola?"

"I hope so," sighed Lola.

Lola left the room to check on the cookies. She returned with a large plateful of butterfly cookies and a bowl of icing. "Let's ice the cookies then take up watch again."

Once they had finished icing, they proceeded to eat one cookie each. "Jasmine wouldn't mind if we ate one, would she?" remarked Miya, stuffing the cookie into her mouth.

As the girls patiently watched the stillness and darkness of the park, they talked about their pets and how amazing it would be if they could communicate with them like Jasmine and the Butterfly Girls did. As the time passed, they all began to feel rather sleepy. Emily looked at her watch, "It's 11pm," she yawned.

Just then a flash appeared in the sky.
What was that?
Did you see it?
Yes, I did.
"Me too," said Lola.

The three little faces woke from their
sleepiness and stared out of the window.

Eyes wide open, waiting, hoping, wishing Butterfly Girl would appear, but as the time passed and there was no sign of Jasmine, they came to the conclusion it must have been a shooting star.

Disappointed yet again, they managed to stay awake another hour, pushing sleepy thoughts from their minds and telling themselves she will appear. But Miya and Emily could no longer keep their eyes open and crawled reluctantly into bed.

Lola gazed out the window one last time, wondering why Jasmine had not turned up. Her head dropped into her hands, and she began to cry. Had it all been a dream?

Chapter Three

Lola sat bolt upright, THE POD BAG!! she remembered.

How could I forget such a special gift from Jasmine, she thought. She jumped

up and pulled the pod bag out from the secret drawer in her desk.

Lola held it tight to her chest; she could almost feel Jasmine's presence. Lola had a feeling, the same kind of feeling she had before she met Jasmine for the first time.

Somehow Jasmine was trying to communicate with her. There was a reason why she couldn't come, thought Lola.

Wiping the tears from her eyes, Lola felt the urge to open the pod bag, which was made from scrap velvets and satin and decorated with sparkling beads that Amber had made. Opening the bag, she noticed a small pocket inside. Taking a closer look, she spotted something pointed hiding inside.

Lola carefully squeezed her small fingers into the pocket and pulled out the mysterious object. She carefully held it in her hand and, to get a better look, lifted it towards the lamp sitting on her desk. As she held it, a tingling sensation ran down her arm and through her body.

It was a crystal. A magical crystal like the ones Jasmine had on her magical pod stick.

Lola carefully put the magic crystal back in the pod bag and climbed into bed cuddling her pod bag. At last, she knew Jasmine would make contact soon. Within minutes, Lola was fast asleep, dreaming of flying with Jasmine once again.

Chapter Four

Miya was first to open her eyes and decided to wake the others with a pillow fight. **WHACK! SPLAT!**

Miya whirled her pillow toward Lola who was still fast asleep under her bedcovers. Then turning quickly, Miya whacked Emily before she could get out of her sleeping bag.

Both Emily and Lola woke up in shock.

"HEY!" they shouted, grabbing their pillows for revenge. Giggling and

ducking, they chased each other around
the room, jumping on the bed and
laughing so much they became entangled

in their sleeping bags.

The more they whacked each other, the more they laughed, finally chasing each other out of Lola's room and into the hall.

All the commotion had woken up the puppy who lunged for Lola's pillow, pulling at it with its teeth. As Lola pulled one way and Prince pulled the other, the pillow burst open, spreading feathers flying everywhere. This of course caused the girls to erupt into another fit of laughter. They watched as all the feathers floated down like snow falling in slow motion. "Quick," giggled Lola, "into my room before my mum and dad wake up," picking up the majority of the scattered feathers as she tiptoed.

They crept back into the bedroom

where Lola declared she had something to show them. Sitting on the bed, Emily and Miya wondered what it could be. Lola walked over to the girls and presented the beautiful pod bag to them.

"WOW, that's gorgeous," said Emily.

Miya's mouth was wide open, "It's amazing!" she eventually managed to say, reaching out to touch it. "Where did you get it? Is it something to do with Jasmine?"

"Yes, it was a gift from Jasmine. She

gave it to me in the Little Humbug Forest."

"WOW, so she really does exist. So why didn't she turn up last night? Why can't we see her?"

"I don't know. Something is wrong, I know that. Look what I found inside the pod bag. Lola opened up the bag and took the crystal out from the pocket. "It's a magic crystal, and it can take us to Jasmine. I'm sure of it!"

"Let's get dressed and go into the garden before anyone gets up."

It was still very early, only 6 am. They couldn't get dressed quickly enough. "Wait for me," shouted Emily, as she scrambled to grab her hair band.

Running out as fast as they could, they realised they weren't wearing any shoes. "You won't need them. The Little Humbugs go barefoot most of the time," announced Lola.

The grass felt damp from the dew, but the air was still warm in the last days of summer.

Remembering how Jasmine held her crystals, Lola placed her magic crystal tightly in her right hand and told the girls to join hands. Immediately as their hands touched, they felt the tingling sensation that Lola had experienced. They felt a power run through them.

"WOW!" said Miya. "Can you feel that?"

"Yes," said Emily excitedly.

In a calm voice, Lola told them they must believe. They had to really want to see Jasmine or she wouldn't appear. They all closed their eyes tightly and thought only of seeing Jasmine. The power grew stronger, and the wind began to blow, whirling and swirling around them, creating a mini whirlwind that whipped their hair into their faces. Suddenly a flash appeared above their heads, and millions of tiny little stars floated around them. Opening their eyes, they

were amazed to see the most beautiful Butterfly Girl fluttering above them.

Her stunning wings sparkled so brightly as the rising sun appeared from behind a cloud. Jasmine had arrived at last.

"Come, I will take you to the Little Humbugs Forest," Jasmine said softly, lifting up her pod stick high into the air and spinning it around and around. The girls could hear the magic crystals smashing against each other as the pod stick spun above them. The sound was almost deafening.

Holding onto Jasmine, they began to lift off the ground, and within seconds they were flying.

"I can't believe it," said Miya. "We are actually flying."

Emily looked down, watching Lola's house getting smaller and smaller the higher they flew. She was speechless trying to take it all in and just held on tight, watching in amazement.

The girls giggled and laughed with Jasmine as they flew through the warm air. The sun was much higher now, catching Jasmine's antennae and making them sparkle like diamonds.

Approaching the Little Humbugs Forest, Miya and Emily spotted the colourful pod homes Lola had told them about. They were just as she had described: bright and colourful egg-shaped pods sticking

out of the forest ground. They looked like such fun places to live, thought Miya.

"Prepare to land," announced Jasmine. "Just watch your bare feet; sometimes these pine needles can spike you." The ground was covered in a carpet of fallen pine needles.

Landing safely, they heard giggles from behind the trees. Then without warning, lots of differently coloured Butterfly Girls ran excitedly to greet the human girls. Wings of all colours fluttered in front of them like dancing flowers in the wind. There were green and blue Butterfly Girls, pink and red, orange and yellow, purple and white, brown and cream, a carnival of colour.

"Hello," they all spoke at once, sounding like a chorus, then bursting into laughter again. This in turn sent Emily, Lola and Miya into fits of giggles, too.

Chapter Five

Miya and Emily had to pinch themselves to make sure they weren't dreaming. It was hard to believe that here they were surrounded by the most beautiful Butterfly Girls, all wanting to meet them.

Jasmine took Miya and Emily's hands, with Lola following behind and introduced them to the Butterfly Girls. The Butterfly Girls we're so excited to see Lola again and to meet her best friends.

The Butterfly Girls were very curious about the human girls and wanted to ask them so many questions. Jasmine was eager to explain to the girls why she had not been able to meet them last night, but she said it would keep until they had

met everyone.

Lucy the Bird Keeper was the first to introduce herself. She looked after all the birds and squirrels of the forest. She knew every species of bird from the largest eagle with a wingspan of two metres to the smallest hummingbird the size of a large insect.

Amber came up next, greeting each girl with a beautiful beaded necklace. She was very artistic and made beads

from the wood of fallen trees.

After nearly every storm, there are usually several fallen trees. The wood is then painted, some used for bird boxes and odd pieces of furniture, explained Amber to Emily and Miya.

Amber also loved to dance and desperately wanted the human girls to

watch the Butterfly Girls dance later that evening.

Lola remembered Chou from her last visit, so she introduced her to Emily and Miya. Chou had potions for every cold and illness the Girls suffered, and she made the most lovely smelling perfumes, too.

Nika arrived late. She had been hunting for gem stones but had no luck; however, she had found some interesting pebbles instead. Nika loved hunting for things and wanted to take the human girls down to the river's edge to look for more stones. However, Jasmine knew they didn't have a lot of time and really wanted them to see the damage that had been caused to part of the forest. It was this damage that had delayed Jasmine visiting Lola last night.

Jasmine had a very special friend to show the human girls.

It was Baby Bee, hiding shyly behind Lucy who had been looking after him.

Lola hadn't met Baby Bee on her first visit to the Humbug Forest and was intrigued as to who he was and why there was only one Baby Bee yet there was lots of Dragonfly Boys and lots more Butterfly Girls.

Jasmine began to explain what had happened to part of the forest where the Humbug Bees lived. It was a small part of the Great Forest in the southern region where the bees fed only on one specific plant – the Nettlenog.

But when that part of the forest was cut down two days ago, all the Humbug Bees died because they could not survive without the Nettlenog.

Some may have flown away, but what would they live on? No one is sure if they would survive.

We only just received the news last night, so we flew the 30 miles south to see if there was anything we could do to help but we had arrived too late. The forest was bare and silent. We were just about to leave when Lucy heard a cry coming from the scattered branches that lay across the dead forest floor. She reached down and moved a branch, revealing a very frightened little Baby Bee. Lucy gently picked him up

and reassured him she was here to help him. Stroking him to calm his nerves, she placed him gently in her arms to keep him safe on their flight home. On our return home we were worried he would not survive because we did not have the Nettlenog plant. However, Chloe the

gardener knew of a plant that was very similar and went at once to fetch some leaves.

Chloe and Lucy have been looking after Baby Bee, who seems to be thriving on Chloe's vegetables and fruit salads mixed with his special leaves. It's early days, but we feel really confident he's going to be fine.

Chapter Six

"Come, girls, I want you to see for yourselves what damage has been done to the forest." They flew 30 miles south of the Little Humbugs Forest where the Humbug Bees lived. This part of the forest was where the Little Humbugs made their very famous, delicious dark honey and produced all the beeswax candles. The Little Humbugs used lots of candles throughout the year; they didn't have electricity.

NOW NOTHING REMAINED.

There was a real sadness in the air.

As they approached the forest, there was a sense of eeriness. It was dead and silent.

The girls couldn't believe how

soundless it was — a disturbing silence.

No bird song, no animals, no colour,
no sweet-smelling wildflowers. Just
a mass of tree stumps and branches
scattered over the ground like debris.
This was such a contrast to the forest
they had just left with its beautiful tall
pine trees, the rich red bark glowing as
the sun beamed through the spiky green
canopy filled with birdsong and life.

Jasmine explained that if the humans

keep cutting down the forests there will
be no shelter, no food, no homes for the
birds and the animals of the forest. Some
may find homes in other parts of the
remaining forests, but others need certain
trees or plants or insects to enable them
to survive, just like Baby Bee.

The girls were saddened by what they

heard and saw. They did not realise
that so many trees had been cut down.
As they stepped over the demolished
Bee hives, they imagined how beautiful
and full of colour this part of the forest
must have been before the life had been
ripped out of it.

They knew they had to help the Little
Humbugs. They were going to make a
difference. As they spoke with a sense
of purpose, they smiled. Holding hands,
they raised their arms high and shouted
at the top of their voices, "We are going
to make a difference."

WE ARE GOING TO MAKE A DIFFERENCE, echoed around the empty forest.

WE ARE GOING TO MAKE A DIFFERENCE

We are going to help the Little Humbugs!

Chapter Seven

Upon their return, they were greeted by Olivia and Chloe, who were a welcome sight after their long flight. Olivia had made a delicious carrot

cake for the girls using Chloe's freshly picked carrots from the Little Humbug vegetable gardens. Carrot cake was a big favourite with everyone. When Olivia wasn't reading, she could be found helping Chloe in the kitchens, baking something yummy for all the Little Humbugs. Olivia was quite

shy. Speaking with a soft voice, she explained to Lola, Miya and Emily how the Little Humbugs live off the land and the sea. Chloe invited them into the very large vegetable gardens and continued into even larger orchards. They had every kind of fruit tree you could ever imagine: peach, plum, pear, orange, lemon, fig and cherry. They even had walnut and

almond trees.

As they walked down the long tree avenues, Chloe noticed several Dragonfly Boys hiding behind one of the old gnarled walnut trees.

"Out you come, Flint," demanded

Chloe. The Head Dragonfly Boy was eager to talk with the human girls.

Flint wanted to explain the Dragonfly's work in the orchards. Chloe rolled her eyes. "We don't work in these orchards; we fly further south where it is more tropical. This is where the Little Humbugs

grow their cocoa trees, banana, coconut and mango."

Lola, Miya and Emily's eyes all lit up. They knew chocolate was made from cocoa and listened eagerly to Flint.

"The cocoa trees like humid tropical climates," explained Flint to his captivated audience. "Further south it is much warmer, and it rains more. Any frost would kill the trees so we have to keep a watchful eye on them over winter. The Dragonfly Boys fly down to harvest the cocoa pods between March and June. The pods are cut from the tree using our long sticks, like this one," he said, holding it up high to let the girls have a closer look.

"Once the pods are harvested, we cut them open and remove the beans. We then place the beans into wooden boxes, cover them with banana leaves and allow them to dry. Once they are dried, the

Dragonfly Boys grind them into powder and store the cocoa powder in wooden barrels. We then transport the barrels up to the Butterfly Girls who use the cocoa to make the most delicious chocolate goodies."

The girls lick their lips; they just loved anything chocolaty.

"In June the Little Humbugs hold their chocolate festival to celebrate the harvest of the cocoa beans. They make everything you could possibly imagine from chocolate. It is one of the best times of the year to be in the forest.

You must come back and visit us during the festival."

The girls totally agreed, "That's a date!" they declared excitedly.

Flint could see his Dragonfly Boys were patiently waiting to play, so he bid the human girls farewell and hoped he would have the pleasure of meeting them again later in the day.

The girls smiled and waved as Flint buzzed so speedily into the distance, creating a short burst of wind with his large transparent wings.

Chloe giggled to herself, knowing Dragonfly Boy was showing off to the girls. She walked them back through the orchards and over to a large field. "We also grow cereals, grains and pulses here," she said, stopping to say hello to a family of bunnies running across the field.

As they made their way back to the centre of the forest, she explained to the human girls that the Little Humbugs only take what they need from the land and the sea and are continually giving back to nature.

"We have chickens that provide us with eggs, and we catch fish from the sea." She explained they had a balance with Mother Nature, and they respected it.

"We gather fresh drinking water from the great spring deep in the forest and collect rainwater for washing. Each Humbug home has its own tub for collecting rainwater, although this year, this part of the forest has hardly had any rain. It has been one of the driest springs and summers ever," sighed Chloe.

Chapter Eight

After their tour of the Humbug village, they ended up at one of the wood-burning ovens, which the Dragonfly Boys made out of clay bricks. Placed all around the forest, these ovens allowed the Little Humbugs to eat outdoors from early spring till the first days of snowfall.

Every Friday Olivia and Chloe would bake pizzas in the ovens for everyone. They ate them outside while being entertained by each other, performing, singing, playing a tune or acting out a play. Although it wasn't Friday, Olivia thought it would be fun for the girls to help her make some pizzas. As they did so, the Little Humbugs entertained them.

All the Butterfly Girls were very musical. They all learned to play the flute and the pipes together a long time ago. These instruments are carefully carved out of recycled wood by Hannah and Una, then rubbed down with beeswax for a nice smooth finish.

Jasmine, Tanya, Amber and Lucy made
their way to the open-air amphitheatre
to play their guitars. The Butterfly Girls
are accompanied by the Dragonfly Boys.
Even Baby Bee feels
brave enough to play the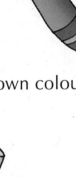
Humbug shaker, a broad
piece of bamboo filled
with dry rice and sealed
at either end. (The Girls
liked to decorate the
Humbug shaker in their own colours.)

With everyone playing, the sound was electrifying. Lola, Emily and Miya were handed Humbug shakers by Amber who was desperate for the human girls to join in. Delighted to be involved, they

jumped up and danced with Amber and the other Butterfly Girls, shaking their Humbug instruments in time to the music, giggling so much their stomachs ached. This was so much fun, having the

most delicious pizzas and being special
guests of the Little Humbugs.

They huddled around the warmth of
the ovens, cooking marshmallows on the
last embers. As it grew darker, the forest
was lit with lanterns that twinkled like
sparkling fairy lights and jewels.

A flash of wings buzzed before them.
It was Flint with some gifts for the girls.

He reached into his secret pocket and
pulled out three beautiful little parcels
individually tagged.

"I knew how much you love chocolate,
so I thought you might like to try these
adorable chocolates we made earlier
this week." The girls were thrilled and
thanked Flint for his very thoughtful gift.

This was such a magical night that
Emily, Lola and Miya didn't want it to
ever end but knew they had to return
home. They said their goodbyes to all
the Little Humbugs, thanking them for
sharing their enchanting world and their

ways with them.

"We have learned so much. It has been so much fun," said the girls.

Jasmine lifted her pod stick in the air, swirling it around their heads faster and faster. Holding hands tightly, they were off before they even had time to blink. The flight home seemed quicker, almost too quick, they felt. They wished the night would never end.

Once they were safely on the ground, Jasmine said, "Do not be sad. This is just the beginning of a wonderful and long-lasting friendship. I will be in touch very soon. Look after your magic crystal," she whispered to Lola. "You never know when you might need it."

The girls smiled and waved goodbye, running into the house before being spotted by Lola's parents.

The girls quickly began work on their

plans to help the Little Humbugs. Their minds were buzzing, filled with so many ideas.

Lola painted a tree on a sheet of paper and wrote above it "WHY TREES ARE SO SPECIAL" and listed all the reasons below.

"We'll put this up in our school for all the kids to see," said Lola.

Just then, Lola's mother popped her head round the door and asked, "So what have you been up to, girls?"

"Oh, just painting and things. Look, we've made this poster for school," said Lola proudly.

After glancing over the text, her mother said, "That's a great idea, girls, well done. Now lights out — don't want you going home exhausted, or your parents won't let you come over for a weekend sleepover ever again." She closed the bedroom door behind her.

The girls started to giggle as they jumped into bed.

"I can't stop thinking about the Little Humbugs."

"Me neither," smiled Miya.

"I know," said Emily "It's my little sister's birthday next week. Why don't we get her a tree? She loves to collect petals in the spring, just like Chou the Butterfly Girl."

"We should get her a cherry blossom tree then," declared Lola.

"That's a great idea," cheered Emily and Miya.

They drifted off to sleep after an incredibly exciting

day, happy that they were helping Jasmine and all the Little Humbugs look after Mother Nature and the environment. As the girls slept soundly, Jasmine secretly fluttered outside Lola's bedroom window, taking one last look at them. She was filled with joy and hope, knowing these girls would make a difference.

Watching them sleep, Jasmine also hoped one day she could enter their world and experience their life.

...Now that's another story!

There is a Butterfly Girl Missing...Is it YOU ?

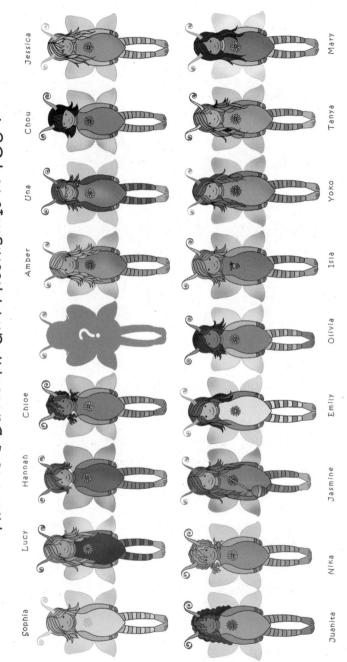

The Butterfly Girl Collection

Coming Soon - Book Three

Discover ...

...the Magical World
of the
Butterfly Girls

The Little Humbug Series

Book Three

It's Cool to Care

Visit Jasmine and all her Butterfly Girl friends at
www.littlehumbugs.com

Check out Jasmine's TV website at
www.littlehumbugs.tv

A special thanks to Patsy Baker and Katrina MacPherson

Remember to find the secret
code in this book to unlock the
special features on the
Little Humbugs website.
The secret code spells the name
of a tree. The code is hidden
in one of the illustrations.

BIRCH   MAPLE   OAK

ELM   ROWAN   PINE

Which tree is the secret code?

www.littlehumbugs.com
Visit the website and click on Book Features

About the
Author/Illustrator

Marghanita Hughes

Marghanita grew up in the Scottish countryside.
She trained as a Graphic Designer in Edinburgh. In 2003
Marghanita wrote and illustrated her first picture book series
'Toffee the Highland Cow'.

In 2005 Marghanita and her family moved half way around
the world to British Columbia. It was watching her own
children at one with nature in their new surroundings that
sparked off the idea for the Little Humbugs.
Marghanita believes that children have an important role to
play in looking after our natural heritage. "My mission is to
get children interested in looking after Mother Nature using
my book characters as positive role models in a fun and
enchanting way".
She lives near a forest with her husband, three children and
Prince, their Flatcoat Retriever.

Keep up to date on all the Little Humbug News.
Visit the website for Butterfly Girl Events
and Book Tours.

www.littlehumbugs.com

WILDWOOD
PRODUCTIONS
PUBLISHING